GOOD-BYE, FOX

written by Catherine James
illustrated by Kenneth Spengler

HARCOURT BRACE & COMPANY
Orlando Atlanta Austin Boston San Francisco Chicago Dallas New York
Toronto London

There goes the fox!

3

Quick! Jump over the gate.

Jump over the mud.

Jump over the rocks.

Jump over the cat!

There goes the fox!
Good-bye fox!